A Note to Parents and Caregivers:

Read-it! Joke Books are for children who are moving ahead on the amazing road to reading. These fun books support the acquisition and extension of reading skills as well as a love of books.

Published by the same company that produces *Read-it!* Readers, these books introduce the question/answer and dialogue patterns that help children expand their thinking about language structure and book formats.

When sharing joke books with a child, read in short stretches. Pause often to talk about the meaning of the jokes. The question/answer and dialogue formats work well for this purpose and provide an opportunity to talk about the language and meaning of the jokes. Have the child turn the pages and point to the pictures and familiar words. When you read the jokes, have fun creating the voices of characters or emphasizing some important words. Be sure to reread favorite jokes.

There is no right or wrong way to share books with children. Find time to read with your child, and pass on the legacy of literacy.

Adria F. Klein, Ph.D.
Professor Emeritus
California State University
San Bernardino, California

Editor: Christianne Jones
Designer: Joe Anderson
Creative Director: Keith Griffin
Editorial Director: Carol Jones
Managing Editor: Catherine Neitge
Page Production: Picture Window Books
The illustrations in this book were created digitally.

Picture Window Books
5115 Excelsior Boulevard
Suite 232
Minneapolis, MN 55416
877-845-8392
www.picturewindowbooks.com

Printed in the United States of America.

Library of Congress Cataloging-in-Publication Data
Ziegler, Mark, 1954-
Wacky workers : a book of job jokes / by Mark Ziegler ; illustrated by
Ryan Haugen.
p. cm. – (Read-it! joke books–supercharged!)
ISBN 1-4048-1164-8 (hardcover)
1. Work–Juvenile humor. I. Haugen, Ryan, 1972- II. Title. III. Series.

PN6231.W644Z54 2006
818'.602–dc22   2005004072

Wacky Workers

A Book of Job Jokes

by Mark Ziegler   illustrated by Ryan Haugen

Special thanks to our advisers for their expertise:

Adria F. Klein, Ph.D.
Professor Emeritus, California State University
San Bernardino, California

Susan Kesselring, M.A.
Literacy Educator
Rosemount–Apple Valley–Eagan (Minnesota) School District

PiCTURE WiNDOW BOOKS
Minneapolis, Minnesota

Customer: "Waiter, there's a twig in my soup!"

Waiter: "Yes, our restaurant has branches everywhere."

Where do math teachers eat?
At the lunch counter.

Why was the baker so rich?

She had a lot of dough.

Why was the garbage collector so sad?

He was down in the dumps.

Customer: "Waiter, this soup tastes funny."

Waiter: "Then why aren't you laughing?"

Why did the accountant have sore feet?

He was working on income "tacks."

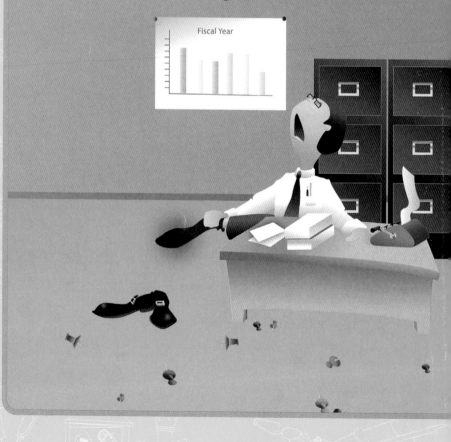

Why did the plumber fall asleep at work?

His job was draining.

Who always starts her job by stopping?

A bus driver.

Customer: "Waitress, do you have chicken legs?"

Waitress: "No. I've always walked like this."

Why did the computer programmer sneeze?
  He had a virus.

Why was the lawyer in and out of the courtroom so fast?

She had a "briefcase."

Why did the police officer stay in bed all day?

He was an undercover cop.

Customer: "Waiter, there's an insect in the butter!"

Waiter: "Yes, we call that a butterfly."

Why did the painter get so hot?
He kept putting on another coat.

**What person always falls
down on the job?**

A paratrooper.

**Why did the comedian
go to the doctor?**

He was feeling a little funny.

Customer: "Waiter, do you have any lobster tails?"

Waiter: "Yes, we do. Once upon a time, there was a little lobster ..."

What nail doesn't a carpenter like to hit?

His fingernail.

Why did the lazy kid work at the shoe store?

She was a loafer.

How did the human cannonball lose his job?

He was fired.

What did the electrician drive to work?

A Volts wagon.

What do you call someone who makes faces all day?

A clock maker.

Customer: "Waiter, there's a bee in my alphabet soup!"

Waiter: "And I'm sure there's an A, a C, and all the other letters, too."

Why did the carpenter stop making wooden cars?

They wooden go.

Why did the firefighter wear stilts to work?

He wanted a raise.

What are a plumber's favorite shoes?

Clogs.

Customer: "Waiter, is there soup on the menu?"

Waiter: "Not anymore. I wiped it off."

Why did the engineer go to locomotive school?

He needed training.

Customer: "Waiter, do you serve crabs here?"

Waiter: "We serve everybody."

Why was the mail carrier so soggy?

She had postage "dew."

Why did the reporter order an ice-cream cone?

He wanted to get the scoop.

Why was the mattress salesman fired?

He was caught lying down on the job.

Customer: "Waiter, can I order the same thing I had yesterday?"

Waiter: "Of course not, you ate it already."

What job has its ups and downs?

A roller coaster operator.

Who gets the most respect in a kindergarten class?

The teacher. All her students look up to her.

Whose job is always looking up?

An astronomer.

Customer: "Waiter, can I eat anything on the menu?"

Waiter: "No, you'll have to eat it on a plate."

Why didn't the butcher sell lunch meat?

He thought it was a bunch of bologna.

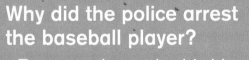

Why did the police arrest the baseball player?

Because he stole third base.

Why did the gravedigger quit his job?

He was tired of the "hole" business.

Read-it! Joke Books— Supercharged!

Beastly Laughs: A Book of Monster Jokes by Michael Dahl

Chalkboard Chuckles: A Book of Classroom Jokes by Mark Moore

Chitchat Chuckles: A Book of Funny Talk by Mark Ziegler

Creepy Crawlers: A Book of Bug Jokes by Mark Moore

Critter Jitters: A Book of Animal Jokes by Mark Ziegler

Fur, Feathers, and Fun! A Book of Animal Jokes by Mark Ziegler

Giggle Bubbles: A Book of Underwater Jokes by Mark Ziegler

Goofballs! A Book of Sports Jokes by Mark Ziegler

Lunchbox Laughs: A Book of Food Jokes by Mark Ziegler

Mind Knots: A Book of Riddles by Mark Ziegler

Nutty Names: A Book of Name Jokes by Mark Ziegler

Roaring with Laughter: A Book of Animal Jokes by Michael Dahl

School Kidders: A Book of School Jokes by Mark Ziegler

Sit! Stay! Laugh! A Book of Pet Jokes by Michael Dahl

Spooky Sillies: A Book of Ghost Jokes by Mark Moore

Wacky Wheelies: A Book of Transportation Jokes by Mark Ziegler

What's up, Doc? A Book of Doctor Jokes by Mark Ziegler

Looking for a specific title or level? A complete list
of *Read-it!* Readers is available on our Web site:
www.picturewindowbooks.com

24